For Mathis and Lilian
For Melinda

First published in the United States, Great Britain, Canada, Australia
and New Zealand in 2008 by North-South Books Inc.,
an imprint of NordSüd Verlag AG, Zürich, Switzerland.
Distributed in the United States by North-South Books Inc., New York.

Library of Congress Cataloging-in-Publication Data is available.
ISBN13: 978-0-7358-2175-0 (trade edition).
Printed in Belgium.
1 3 5 7 9 10 8 6 4 2

www.northsouth.com

Loopy

BY AURORE JESSET

ILLUSTRATED BY BARBARA KORTHUES

NorthSouth
BOOKS

NEW YORK/LONDON

I left my Loopy at the doctor's.

I need to go back and get him RIGHT NOW!

But Mommy says it's too late.

She says we can get Loopy tomorrow.

Tomorrow is too late.

I need my Loopy RIGHT NOW!

Mommy says I should sleep with another toy tonight.

But another toy is not the same.

Another toy is not my Loopy.

What if another child finds Loopy?

What if he twirls Loopy around too hard,
or pulls his ears,
or takes him home forever?

What if he throws Loopy into the garbage?

Then the garbage truck will come and eat him up!

Or what if nobody finds Loopy?
What if he has to spend all night alone in the dark
with the doctor's office ghosts?
He will be so frightened.
I have to save him!

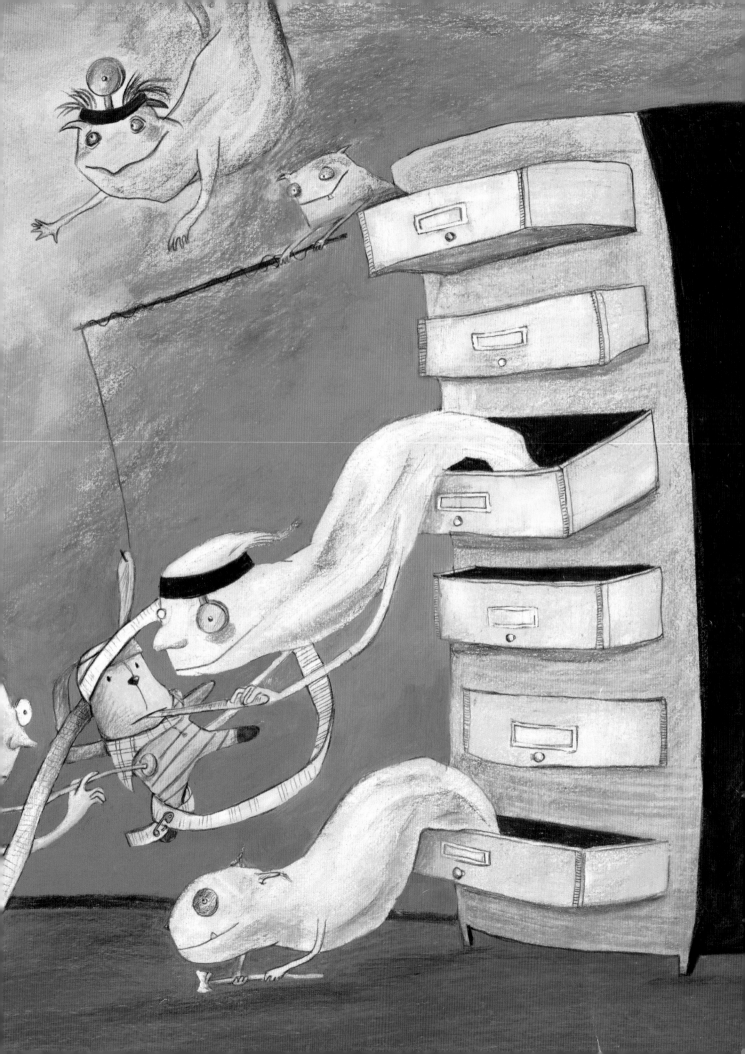

I will rescue Loopy
all by myself.

I won't tell Mommy.
I think I know the way.

But what if I get lost?

What if no one will help me?

What if a grumpy giant finds me

and carries me into a dark forest?

What if he puts me in his basement?
Would there be bugs and spiders?
Giants probably like bugs and spiders.

BRRRIIIIIIIIING

It's the doorbell!

Someone is at the door.

I see someone through the glass.

He is holding something with long ears!

It's LOOOOOOOOOPY!

The doctor found him in the waiting room.

He knew right away that I needed my Loopy.

Were you frightened, Loopy?

I was going to rescue you!

Everything is all right now.
Oh, Loopy!
I'm so glad you're home!

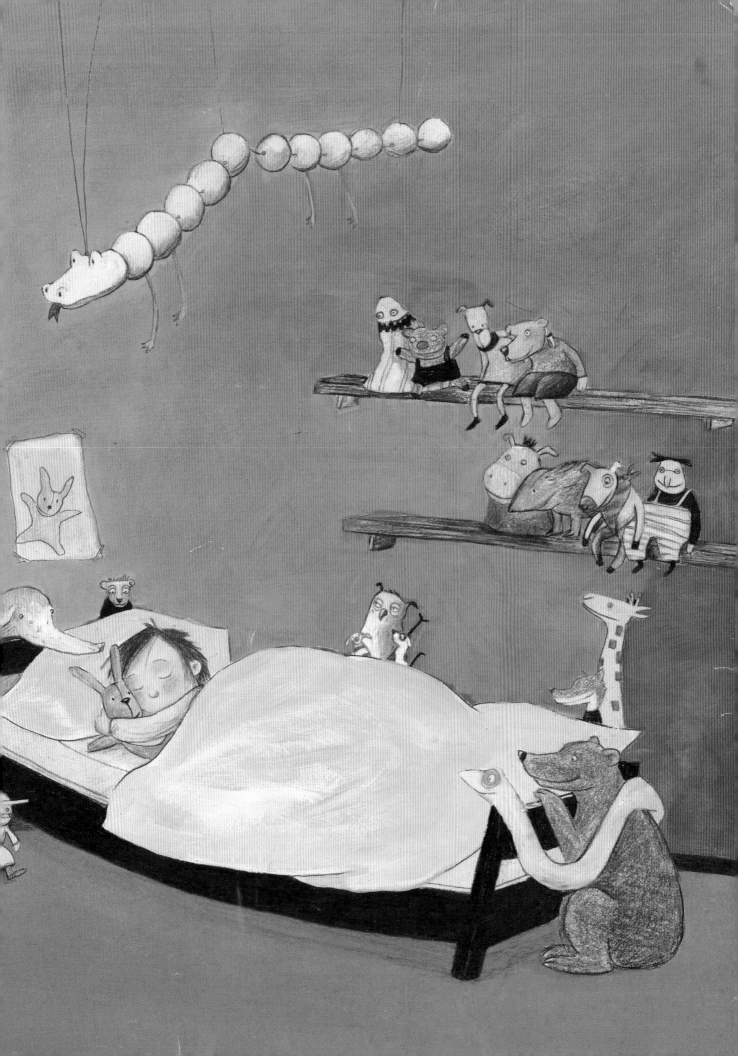